CALUM'S
HARD KNOCKS

D1645713

For Barbara – D.S.

To François for being so patient while I spent
so much time with Calum :) – A.A.M.

Young Kelpies is an imprint of Floris Books
First published in 2016 by Floris Books

The publisher acknowledges subsidy from
Creative Scotland towards the publication
of this volume

This book is also
available as an eBook

British Library CIP data available
ISBN 978-178250-280-7
Printed in Great Britain by Bell & Bain ltd

CALUM'S HARD KNOCK

written by **Danny Scott**

illustrated by **Alice A. Morentorn**

Young Kelpies

CALUM
FERGUSON

ERIKA
BROWN

LEWIS BUDGE

LEO
NKWANU

JANEK POWOLSKI

FRASER MCDONALD

LEIGHTON

RAVI GUPTA

JORDAN MCPRIDE

King's
Park Athletic

Jordan's house

Caleytown
shopping centre

Fraser's house

Park

Leo's house

Scouts and Shouts

At morning break Calum could tell something wasn't right.

He crossed the playground of Caleytown Primary with his friends Fraser and Leo. They were heading towards the Astroturf pitches. Jordan McPride's crew, Ravi, Ryan and Lewis, were already there, staring at them.

Jordan had a brand new football under one foot and his arms were crossed. He smirked at them and whispered something into his friend

Lewis's ear. The tough midfielder nodded his red head back and forth and rearranged his freckled face into a big grin.

Ravi, Caleytown's goalkeeper, carried out some essential maintenance on his incredible quiff, and tall, wiry Ryan just kind of stood there, quiet as ever.

Calum's friend Leo, on the other hand, hadn't noticed that anything was up. He was too busy telling Fraser a funny story from the October break. "My dad took me and Calum to Wateradventure!"

"I've heard the flumes there are massive!" Fraser said, all wide-eyed.

"They are, they are. You can go as fast as a car down them. But..." Leo held up a finger, "if you know what you're doing, you can slow yourself down and wait for your mates to catch up."

Calum winced. He knew what was coming next.

"Calum didn't know!" Leo yelled. "He's never been before! So when he came round the corner and saw me, he screamed like I was some kind of sea monster and crashed right into me!"

Fraser collapsed into giggles, while Calum checked to see if his ribs were still sore from the collision in the waterslide.

"You left out the part where your dad had to beg the lifeguard not to throw us out," Calum added.

Leo just winked.

"What are you guys so happy about?" Jordan asked as they got nearer. "You're not even scouted yet."

"What?" Calum's brain struggled to change track from water flumes to what happened at the end of Caleytown's last league match: a match they'd won 5–3. Their football hero James Cauldfield had come to see them play, and he'd brought along a scout from his team, King's Park Athletic. Everyone had seen the scout talking to Calum and Leo afterwards, but only Jordan had taken it personally.

"My dad said the scout *might* watch you again for next year's under-12s," Jordan said. "So you're not scouted yet, big head."

"Er... I know," said Calum.

Jordan popped his collar and looked round to make sure he had everyone's attention. "My dad used to play for King's..."

"...Park Athletic. You've told us before," Leo interrupted. "About five hundred times?"

Fraser giggled again. Jordan shut the P5 up with a stare.

"Whatever, you're just jealous cause your dad only takes X-rays for a living." Jordan raised his hand to dismiss Leo. "Anyway, *my* dad said if the scout had thought you were *that* good – *which you're not* – he would've scouted you right there and then."

Lewis and Ravi nodded enthusiastically, like they were getting paid to agree with their friend.

"Just cause the scout wasn't talking to *you*, McPride,"

Leo fired back, "you're acting like a total McIdiot."

Fraser stood planted to the spot, staring up at the P6s. His big eyes switched from Jordan's crew back to his own crew, Calum and Leo.

"Whatever." Jordan picked up his ball. "Right guys, let's play some seven-byes."

"Jeez, finally," Leo sighed and took a step forward with Calum and Fraser.

Jordan's hand shot up and stopped them in their tracks. "What are *you* doing?" he pointed a finger at them. "I don't want you big heads playing with my new ball. You might burst it with your... eh, big heads."

"McBaby," Leo said under his breath.

He looked back at Calum and Fraser and shrugged. "No football until training, I guess."

They wandered back to the playground to see what else kids did at break.

Battles

"Listen up, gentlemen. Headteacher Sanderson is coming to watch us take on Battlehill this week," Mr McKlop addressed his squad. "So, I want you guys to show her how much hard work you've put into this team."

Mr McKlop was the coach of Caleytown's P6 team, and he was Calum's teacher too. For training, he had changed out of his usual corduroy suit into a brand new tracksuit. Calum could tell it was new because there was a price tag still attached to the back of the collar.

The coach pushed his floppy hair back off his glasses and looked at his clipboard. "Now, Battlehill haven't conceded a goal all year. Let's change that for them. Get yourself organised in groups of three. Ravi, you're in goal."

The teams sprung into life. After not being able to play football at break, Calum, Leo and Fraser were desperate to score some goals. So desperate, in fact, that it didn't occur to Calum that taking on Jordan's crew might not be such a good idea after their argument.

It only dawned on him that things could turn nasty when he saw a cat-like grin spread across Leo's face as he squared up to Jordan McPride.

Leo did three quick step-overs to put Jordan off balance. Then he faked a pass to Fraser that Jordan bought – hook, line and sinker. The defender lunged to block the ball but Leo dragged it back the other way and slotted it through Jordan's legs. "Nutmeg!"

Jordan fell over in slow motion.

But Leo wasn't finished with him yet.

Ryan and Lewis looked on helplessly as Leo dribbled round their friend. Jordan could only flail at the ball like a fish out of water.

"That's enough, Leo!" Mr McKlop barked. He pushed his glasses up his nose.

Jordan rose to his feet, his eyes never leaving his tormentor.

Later that afternoon Calum was round at Leo's house on Leo's mum's tablet. As usual, they were browsing Scotland Stars, a website dedicated to primary school football.

"You made Jordan look pretty stupid at

training today," Calum said, looking at his friend out the corner of his eye.

"Maybe, but he had it coming to him." Leo shifted on the couch. "Since when was the team all about him anyway?"

"Yeah, I mean, don't get me wrong, it was totally hilarious... but I don't think Mr McKlop was impressed."

"It'll all be forgotten by match day," Leo said through a yawn. "Jordan's got to realise sooner or later that he's being a jealous McIdiot."

"I hope so." Calum was unconvinced.

"Forget about Jordan, Cal. Let's see who we're up against next..." Leo tapped on a link to a profile of Battlehill Primary F.C.

NATIONAL SOCCER SEVENS TOURNAMENT
CENTRAL WILDCATS LEAGUE

MATCH DAY THREE COMING UP:
CALEYTOWN VS BATTLEHILL

REISS ROBERTSON REPORTS

It's going to be second versus third in this tasty-looking encounter.

In the last round of fixtures, surprise guest, King's Park Athletic and Scotland striker James Cauldfield, turned up at Caleytown's home match against St Joseph's. And he had a scout in tow. The scout is rumoured to have approached goalscorers Leo Nkwanu and Calum Ferguson after the game.

But both players might find it harder to hit the net against the impressive Battlehill defence featuring identical twins Nic and Ric Catenaccio. Coached by their father, they have yet to concede a goal this season.

"See," Leo said. "We've got more than Jordan Mc-My-dad-used-to-play-for-King's-Park to worry about."

Calum nodded.

The Catenaccios

For neighbours Calum and Erika, going to Mr Aziz's shop down the road felt like putting on your comfiest clothes.

"How's Scotland's future number nine?" Mr Aziz greeted Calum the next morning. And as Erika followed through the shop door, he added, "Oh, and USA's future keeper too!"

"Ace, thanks!" Calum smiled, feeling instantly better. "It's match day."

Leo burst through the door, out of breath. "Sorry I'm late."

"Lightning Leo! Think you'll beat Battlehill?" Mr Aziz raised an eyebrow.

"Too right," Leo boasted, as he zipped over to the juice fridge. "We're unbeaten at home."

"You've only played two games at home," Erika said flatly.

Mr Aziz giggled.

"Yeah... and we won them both." Leo closed the fridge door. "We are, therefore, unbeaten at home – true fact."

Calum wasn't feeling as confident. "Battlehill haven't let a goal in this year. It says on Scotland Stars that they've got identical twins in defence, and they each seem to know what the other will do before they do it."

"They're telepathic, you mean," Mr Aziz said.

"Tele-what?" Leo asked.

"Telepathic, dummy," Erika jumped in. "It means they can read each other's minds."

"Whatever," Leo said. "They'd better get used to reading 'Caleytown 5 Battlehill 0' on the results page."

Erika sighed and laughed at the same time. Leo had that effect on people.

The rain hammered down on both teams. Caleytown trailed by 1–0 and didn't look as if they would be scoring any time soon.

Up front in his yellow strip, Calum felt like he couldn't get any wetter. And yet, the rain kept pouring. He was desperate to get a goal for his team but Ric and Nic Catenaccio, identical in their blue-and-white stripes, had him running back and forth between them like he was a soaking ball in their own personal tennis match.

It looked like things might change when midfielder Lewis surged into the sodden Battlehill half.

Seeing his first chance in ages, Calum reacted before the twins and opened up some daylight between himself and Ric. Or was it Nic? Regardless, he yelled to Lewis for a pass.

Lewis raised his red head of hair to see Calum in space in the box, but he ignored Calum's shouts. He shot from miles out instead, and his effort was deflected wide for a corner.

"Why didn't you pass?" Calum shouted through the rain.

Lewis shrugged as if to say sorry, but Calum saw him turn and nod at Jordan.

"Ricardo... Niccolo, concentrate!" the twins' dad and team coach shouted from the sideline. He was staying dry under a black umbrella that was keeping the rain off his navy blue coat and sharp black suit.

On the other sideline, Mr McKlop's hair was stuck to the sides of his head, his new tracksuit was soaked through, and he was blowing his nose.

Leo ran to take the corner, while Calum sprinted about in the box, trying to lose Ric and Nic. But the twins followed Calum like bodyguards, leaving Jordan marked by someone half his size.

Leo saw Jordan waving his arms, but ignored him. He launched the ball to Calum instead, who had no chance of getting to it first.

"Stop only passing it to your mates!" Jordan shouted at Leo.

"You and Lewis started it!" Leo shouted back.

A very wet
Mr McKlop stifled
a sneeze and looked
down the sideline
at Headteacher
Sanderson. Under her
school umbrella
her sharp nose was
twitching. She looked
decidedly unimpressed.

As the Battlehill keeper
prepared to kick the ball back down the
pitch, Calum heard the twins laughing behind
his back.

"It's like playing two separate teams."

"Yeah. Two teams of toddlers. How did these guys ever beat Muckleton Primary?"

PEEEEEEEE-EEP!

Calum felt relieved to hear the half-time whistle. Maybe Mr McKlop could tell them how to fix things.

A Rout

"What-ha-ha-CHOO..." Mr McKlop sneezed over the Caleytown players standing in the rain at half-time. "*What*, is going on out the-he-her-ha-CHOO?"

Nobody in yellow spoke. The only sound was rain hitting Astroturf. Even Ravi's normally immaculate quiff had been flattened in the downpour. It made him look much shorter.

"I don't mind that we're losing, it's the lack of teamwork I don't like," Mr McKlop continued.

"The only person here who's playing for the team, and not just their pals, is Janek."

Caleytown's strong central defender stared straight ahead. His sharp blue eyes gave nothing away.

Jordan's expression, on the other hand, gave everything away. His eyes shifted from Leo to Calum to Fraser and back. He was desperate to start pointing fingers.

Calum tried to ignore Jordan's accusing looks and glanced down the sideline at the crowd instead, hoping that a scout hadn't turned up. Because of the rain, the 'crowd' was just their headteacher Mrs Sanderson, Erika Brown and her American mum, who coached the P6 girls' team.

"Right. If no one has any-ay-ay-ay-ha-CHOO," Mr McKlop sneezed again. "Any-*thing* to say for themselves, then get back out there and show me that I'm imagining all your squabbling.

Otherwise, I'll be making some permanent substitutions."

Calum glanced at the substitutes Max, Ewan and Ryan. They all looked like they'd been swimming with their bibs on.

"You'd better pass to us in this half," Jordan whispered behind Leo, Calum and Fraser.

"Oh yeah?! That goes for you too!" Leo hissed back, he shook the water out of his hair and pointed a thumb back at Lewis. "And tell your henchman to try making a run into the box for a change, it'll help us get past the telepathic twosome."

Leo was talking about Ric and Nic Catenaccio, who appeared to be sharing a joke

as they walked back onto the pitch. Somehow, they looked reasonably dry.

The game restarted and Calum soon had Ric and Nic on his tail.

"Did you all kiss and make up at half-time?" Ric, or maybe it was Nic, laughed in Calum's ear.

"Whatever." Calum was getting frustrated. Every time he got away from one of the twins, the other would appear at his shoulder.

Regardless, Leo kept trying to pass to him.

"Ungh! Come on, Leo! Try passing to someone else for a change," Lewis, who was free for a shot, grunted in frustration.

Leo ignored him, dribbled across the pitch and played in Fraser, who ran at Battlehill's goal.

One of the twins sprinted over to tackle Fraser, leaving Calum unmarked for the first time this half!

Calum screamed for a cutback.

Fraser slid the ball to him, but only just before he himself was sent flying through the air by Ric, or was it Nic, Catenaccio.

Even though Lewis was free, Calum kept his eyes on the

football, shaped to shoot and put his laces through it.

THUNK!

It smacked off the post and fell to the one of the twins, who controlled the ball, spun round, and strode down the pitch.

"Tackle him!" Leo shouted at Lewis, who was the closest Caleytown player to the Catenaccio, but Lewis just watched the twin stride away.

Jordan was next in line between the Catenaccio brother and the goal. He sprinted, threw himself to the turf... and slid right past the twin.

"What are you doing?!" Calum heard himself

scream. It looked like Jordan's crew were letting Battlehill through!

Ravi came out of goals but Ric-or-Nic ran round him easily and rolled the ball into the net to double Battlehill's advantage.

"Bravo Niccolo, bravo!" the twins' dad shouted.

"I'm Ricardo, Papà," Ricardo shouted over.

His dad held up a hand to apologise.

Calum wanted an apology too. He was furious. He took a deep breath and was ready to accuse Jordan when he heard Fraser moaning, "Ow, ow, ow", behind him.

Fraser was still on the ground from his collision with Nic. Mr McKlop had run over to help him up.

"Don't put any weight on it-hi-hit-ACHOO!" he said.

Ryan, another one of Jordan's cronies, ran on to replace the injured winger.

"It's just you and me now, Cal." Leo shrugged.

"I guess," Calum said, feeling the cold rain wash his anger away.

Challenge or Bust

"Can anybody tell me what happened out there?"

Mr McKlop had summoned the team to the gym hall after they'd all changed out of their wet kit. Inside, only half the lights were on and the heating was definitely off.

The team lay about like a bunch of broken toys on the gym floor. Fraser held an ice pack against his dead leg.

Caleytown had eventually lost 4–0.

Headteacher Sanderson hadn't even stayed until the end.

"Calum and Leo weren't passing to me and Lewis!" said Jordan, sitting upright.

"You and your crew started it!" Calum shouted, before Leo even had a chance.

Everyone stared at Calum in surprise.

It wasn't like him to get angry, but he wasn't finished yet.

"You even let one of the twins through to score *just* to make me and Leo look bad!"

"No we didn't!" Jordan protested. "I just slid too far, you weirdo."

"HAAACHOOO!" Mr McKlop sneezed so hard his glasses fell off. The noise echoed round the gloomy hall. He picked them up and peered through them to make sure they weren't broken. "I have never been embarrassed as a coach," said Mr McKlop, sliding his glasses back on, "until today."

Calum stared at the wooden floor.

"If you'd been beaten 4–0 but played

your hearts out for each other, I would still be proud of you all-hall-ha-CHOO!" Mr McKlop blew his nose. "I don't know *how* I'll explain this to Headteacher Sanderson." His shoulders slumped. "In fact, if this is the reward I get for giving up my spare time to coach you, I'm not sure it's worth it."

Calum felt his stomach sink like a stone.

"Are you quitting the team?" Leo blurted out.

Mr McKlop stood completely still for a moment before he spoke. "No, Leo. You've all done enough in the past to earn yourselves another chance."

The team shuffled about on the shiny floor. Mr McKlop had their attention now.

"This is what's going to happen," he continued. "On Friday, after school, we're going on a team-building trip."

Calum heard a few of his teammates groaning.

"Fine. Groan all you want." Mr McKlop took a deep breath. "But if you lot aren't willing to sort this mess out, then I'll withdraw Caleytown from the Scotland Stars league." He stood staring at them for a second, then left through the double doors.

"Here they are!" Mr Aziz beamed as Calum, Leo and Erika trudged into his shop. "Will the Battlehill twins be reading 5–0 tonight on Scotland Stars?"

Calum almost managed a smile.

"That good, huh?" Mr Aziz turned the volume down on a Spanish football highlights show.

"We got thumped 4–0 and Mr McKlop said he might quit the team," said Leo.

"What? Why? Because you lost?" Mr Aziz looked confused.

"No," Erika answered for them. "Because the whole team acted like a bunch of babies who didn't want to share their toys."

Mr Aziz tried not to laugh. Leo scowled at Erika. She scowled right back.

Calum started to pick a mix of sweets to cheer himself up.

"It's all Jordan's fault," he said, biting into a jelly snake. "He's jealous because the King's Park Athletic scout spoke to us and not him."

"Yeah," Leo chimed in. "Just 'cause his dad played for the Tigers doesn't mean *he* will."

"That sounds tricky," said Mr Aziz, rubbing his chin. "But you've got to admit, it must be hard for Jordan to try and follow in his father's footsteps..."

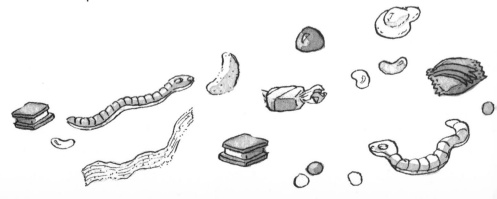

"Especially when he can barely kick a ball straight." Leo grinned and bumped fists with Calum.

Erika rolled her eyes. "*Anyway*, did anyone bother to ask what you're going to do on your team-building trip?"

"No one asked," Leo shrugged.

"You guys are the worst," Erika laughed, shaking her head.

"Whatever he has planned, I hope it works," said Calum.

Elevens

There was no chance Jordan was going to let Calum and Leo play football with his crew at breaktime any more.

Instead, Calum had brought his own ball and invited Erika and her friend Sally to play. Fraser still had a dead leg, so he watched from a bench with some of his P5 friends.

"Are you sure you're happy to be seen playing with *girls*?" Sally's mischievous brown eyes teased the boys from under her dark

fringe. She scraped the rest of her hair into a ponytail.

"Yeah!" Calum and Leo said, trying to ignore Jordan and Ravi laughing at them from up the other end of the pitch.

Erika, for one, was delighted to have any extra opportunity to play football. She started handing out sheets of paper. "Here are some rules for a game I thought the four of us could play."

Leo held the sheet like it was covered in germs. "Wait. Did you make these especially for today?"

"Well… yeah. I wrote them out and my mom photocopied them for me. *Why*?" Erika asked, as if everyone did stuff like that.

Calum stood on Leo's foot to shut him up and buried his head in the rules...

Each player starts with a total of 11 points. They each take it in turns to go in goals. The aim of the game is to work together to take points off whoever is the keeper.

Being the Goalkeeper!

The oldest player must go in goal first, but gets 12 points instead. After that, players must swap with the goalkeeper whenever:

1. their shot, header or volley is caught by the keeper before it bounces...

2. they miss the target completely!

Scoring

You can only lose points when you are the keeper.

You do not gain points by scoring goals.

The number of points you lose depends on what kind of goal your opponent scores. The scoring is as follows:

-1 point if you let in any shot from outside the box

-2 points if you let in a volley

-3 points for letting in a header

-4 points for letting in a back-heeled goal

Winners!

The game ends when a player has lost all their points.
Everyone else wins!

"Unlucky, Leo!" Erika shouted. She had flown to
her left and plucked Leo's ambitious shot out
of the air. "You're in!"

Leo laughed and shook his head. Even though he only had seven points left, he kept trying outrageous volleys.

Sally was tied on eight points with Calum, but Erika was still on ten. The game did suit Erika though – everyone knew she was a great keeper.

"So, do you know where Mr McKlop's taking you for your team-building trip yet?" Sally asked Calum, while flicking the ball up in the air.

Calum got up on his tiptoes ready for Sally's pass. "No idea. The consent form told our parents to pack old trainers, but that was it."

Sally lobbed a pass into Calum's path.
In goals, Leo spread his arms wide.

"My mom told me he was *really* upset after

the Battlehill game," Erika said. "So you guys better go— FINISH IT CALUM!"

Calum bounded forward and flung himself at Sally's pass for a diving header. He connected with the ball and sent it down low where Leo couldn't catch it.

Erika laughed as Leo jumped in the shape of a starfish to try to block it, but it flew in to take three points off Leo's score and put him in goal.

"I think we've finally found a game you're no good at, Leo." Calum grinned. He had landed on the damp ground after his header, leaving wet patches right down his school trousers, but it had been worth it.

"Lucky bounce," Leo said. His score was down to four. "Those are the last points I'm gonna lose today!"

Erika and Sally had different ideas. They started another move, but the bell rang for the end of break.

"BREAKTIME'S OVER, GIRLIES!" Jordan shouted from up the other end of the pitch. Lewis, Ravi and Ryan laughed as if he had made the greatest joke of all time. Janek, who'd joined them for a game, was already crossing the playground.

"I think I'd rather spend Friday afternoon doing homework than spend it with Jordan and that bunch of donuts," Leo said.

"I know," Calum said.

"You'd better find a way to get on, fellas." Erika was firm. "Otherwise you'll have no team to get scouted from."

Sally hooted.

Still in goals, Leo was so busy trying to come up with a smart response that he didn't see Sally turn around and line up a back-heel.

"Save this, Lightning Leo!" she shouted. She kicked her leg back like a donkey to send the ball right past Leo and take his remaining four points.

"Nice!" Calum shouted, despite Leo's grumpy face.

7

Into the Woods

Calum had been on less awkward bus journeys.

It was Friday: the team-building trip. On the back seats, Jordan and his crew sat whispering to each other. Occasionally, they would all turn to look at Calum, Leo or Fraser and laugh.

Janek sat in the middle with Max and Ewan, staring out at the countryside as it rolled past the window.

Leo and Calum sat near the front and tried their best to ignore Jordan's crew, while Fraser,

also up the front, was completely oblivious
to it all. He spent the whole journey chatting
away to their sneezing driver, Mr McKlop.

They drove along a country road past cows, sheep and fields for about twenty minutes before, finally, turning down a rutted lane that led into a wood. Mr McKlop carefully reversed the minibus into a car park pockmarked with muddy puddles.

Lewis, who always got travelsick, barged his way off the bus first. While he stood, green and gulping fresh air, the rest of the boys filed past him into the November chill and stood around stretching and yawning.

"Where on earth are we?" Leo whispered to Calum.

Calum shrugged.

"This way-ay-ah-CHOO!" Mr McKlop walked

towards an arrow pointing through the trees.

The boys quickly fell into three different groups behind him until they all emerged into a damp clearing half-filled with camouflaged tents.

A woman dressed in a green army uniform appeared from the biggest tent. She wore a cap so low on her forehead that it cast a shadow over most of her face, and a long ponytail hung down her back like a rope. Her sewn-on badge said Sergeant McCradge.

"What the...?" Jordan said.

"Atten-TION!" she shouted at them.

A few of the Caleytown squad stumbled back in surprise.

"I said, atten-TION!" Sergeant McCradge stood with her black boots a shoulder-width apart.

The confused team arranged themselves to face the sergeant, trying to copy her stance while slipping about on the muddy ground.

Mr McKlop bit his bottom lip to stop himself from laughing.

"What has Mr McKlop signed us up for?" Calum whispered to Leo.

"I dunno..."

"SILENCE!" Sergeant McCradge glared at Calum and Leo.

Calum could feel Jordan smirking at him to his left.

"LISTEN UP!" The sergeant paced in front of Caleytown's squad. "I hear you lads embarrassed yourselves recently. I *hear* you've been whining and moaning at each other like a bunch of spoilt little brats."

"We sure have, sir... I mean, ma'am," Fraser shouted out.

Everyone shook their heads. Even Sergeant

McCradge took a long, hard look at Fraser to make sure he was for real.

"*Well,* you won't get away with that today. In order to survive this afternoon you'll need TEAMWORK and DISCIPLINE," she boomed. "Welcome... to *Assault Cross.*"

Leo and Calum turned and mouthed *Assault Cross* to each other.

Sergeant McCradge stared hard at each player.

"Today you will be completing one of the toughest assault courses in Scotland.

You will feel the strain in your *muscles...*

You will feel the strain in your *minds...*

You will feel the strain in your *hearts.*"

"I can feel the strain in my ears already," Leo whispered quietly to Calum.

Calum coughed to hide his laugh and drew a hard stare from the sergeant.

She took a deep breath and started up again. "You cannot complete this course in ones and twos. You cannot complete this course in threes and fours. To complete this journey, all ten of you will need to work together."

Calum stole a glance at Jordan. He was silently shaking his head.

"Behind me, in this tent, are your uniforms. Get changed and meet me at the starting line over there in T-minus five minutes."

The squad moved like little kids unsure if

they were allowed to leave the naughty step.

"NOW, gentlemen, MOVE MOVE MOVE!"
Sergeant McCradge made their minds up for
them.

Tyres

Four minutes and fifty-five seconds later, Calum, Leo and Fraser stood with the rest of the team staring out at a small field full of car tyres laid on their sides in the mud. The rest of the assault course snaked off into the woods.

Everyone, apart from Mr McKlop, had changed into green army uniforms and black woollen hats. (Ravi still made every effort to ensure his quiff was on show.)

"You have exactly forty-five minutes to complete this course, boys, otherwise you'll have failed to save this team," Sergeant McCradge shouted before turning to speak into her walkie-talkie. "Private Patterson, do you copy? The eagle has landed. I repeat: the eagle has landed."

Jordan started pushing buttons on his big fancy watch.

"What if it gets wet, Jordan?" asked Ravi. "Aren't you worried you could break it?"

"Hah!" Jordan laughed. "This watch is completely waterproof. They tested it with divers. You can wear it two-hundred metres under the sea. It even reads my heart rate."

"Can it tell you when you're being a boring show off?" Leo asked.

Jordan gave Leo an evil look.

"That's enough-HUFF-HACHOO!" Mr McKlop interrupted the bickering. "Let me remind you that if you don't complete this course *as a team* there will be no more team."

Calum elbowed Leo in the ribs in a way that he hoped would shut him up. No matter how sick he was of Jordan, he wanted more than anything to save the team and stay in the league.

"Right, are you ready, Caleytown?" Sergeant McCradge clipped her walkie-talkie back into her holster and moved her whistle to her lips.

"Wait. What is *that*?" She pointed at Ravi's quiff. "Please get that ridiculous haircut out of my sight, rookie."

Ravi reluctantly tucked his quiff under his hat.

"Can I get the first four runners?"

Jordan, Lewis, Ryan and Ravi made sure they were lined up at the front of the group. They all nodded to each other.

"This tyre run will test your agility, your concentration, and your awareness of those around you. One lapse and you *will* be eating tyre rubber for lunch."

Steam rose from the players' mouths and quivered in the air.

The sergeant hunkered down into a squat. "Three... two... one..."

PEEEEEEEEEEEP!

The ear-splitting noise of McCradge's whistle shocked some crows out of the trees and Caleytown off into the course.

Jordan's crew powered through the tyre run like horses running over a cattle grid. Their shoes sent mud pellets flying everywhere.

Calum, Leo, Fraser and Max watched and waited for their whistle.

PEEEEEEEEP!

Calum clipped the first tyre with his foot but quickly got the hang of the obstacle. The key was to lift your knees high and concentrate on the tyre holes right in front of you. His thighs soon started to ache but Calum was only a few rows behind Fraser, who was catching up to Ryan, fast.

"Hurry up!" Fraser shouted through the mud flicking up into his face from the wingback's shoes.

But Ryan was already at full speed. Fraser had no choice but to put the brakes on.

"Oh, ah, argh!" He shouted, as he clipped a tyre with his right foot, tripped on a tyre with his left, and fell face-first onto the rubber.

"Ha, ha, ha!" Jordan had finished in time to see Fraser fall. He laughed as much as he could while trying to catch his breath. "Way to burn rubber, Fraser. Burn rubber on your face!"

Without saying a word, Fraser jumped straight back up and powered through the rest of the tyres towards them.

Seeing this, Jordan and his three-man crew stopped their cackling and spun on their heels, desperate to ensure they were first in line for the next obstacle.

When Leo, Calum and Fraser tottered over

to join them, their jaws dropped: in front of them was a metre-high drop down into a muddy bog, and hanging over it were two dangling trapeze lines.

Trapeze Artists

"Ready for your next fall, Frazzler?" Jordan offered his hand to Lewis for a fist bump, but Lewis was nervously looking out at the swing bars.

Leo looked like he wanted to shove Jordan off the platform.

"*Lewis,*" Jordan whispered, his fist still hanging in the air. "Lewis Budge!"

"Oh, sorry J." Lewis finally bumped fists. He looked paler than normal.

"You feeling alright, Budgie?" Ravi asked.

"I don't like the look of this. I don't like heights. Don't like them at all."

"Atten-TION!" Sergeant McCradge bellowed, from knee-deep in the bog below them, halfway between the launching and landing platforms. Everyone shuffled round to look down at her.

"Here, you lads will need to swing from where Private Patterson is standing at point A, to Mr McKlop at point B over there." Sergeant McCradge motioned to each point with a rigid finger. "To do so you will need plenty of encouragement from your fellow soldiers."

The whole team seemed to gulp at once, apart from Leo. He was already taking the first bar from Private Patterson, a bored-looking teenager dressed in uniform.

"So, which one of you has the courage to go first?" Sergeant McCradge moved her whistle to her lips.

But it was too late. Leo had already launched himself off the platform and was swinging through the air.

"Hey!" Private Patterson shouted, as Leo caught the next bar and swung safely over the muddy pit to the landing platform.

"Go Leo!" Fraser roared his approval.

Not to be outdone, Ravi caught the swinging bar before the Private could grab it, and flung himself off the platform. He gripped the second bar just like Leo had and landed at point B next to him.

Before Calum could follow suit, Jordan snatched the bar as it swung back. He flung himself over too.

Private Patterson threw his hands up into the air while Sergeant McCradge blew furiously on her whistle from down below.

Calum ignored all the commotion and made sure he was next.

"This is ACE!" Leo said, almost hopping

up and down with excitement when Calum landed beside him. Assault Cross was way more fun than they'd thought it would be.

"Calm down, losers," Jordan scoffed.

Sergeant McCradge gave up blowing her whistle and watched player after player complete the obstacle until only two remained: Lewis and Janek.

"Budgie! You're next!" Ravi shouted across to the launching platform.

Lewis stood with the bar in his hands.

Even in the murky woods Calum could see his lips trembling. Behind him, Janek was waiting patiently for his turn.

Everyone fell silent as they watched Lewis

teeter on the edge of the platform.

"Come on, Lewis!" Leo said. "Before it gets dark."

Mr McKlop shot Leo a look.

"Come on Budgie!" Ravi shouted. "You can do it, man!"

Timidly, Lewis slid forward off the edge. As he swung to the middle of the pit he grabbed the next bar, but didn't have the momentum to get to the landing platform.

"Argh... argh... argh!" Lewis dangled above the muddy pit.

"Kick your legs, Budgie!" Ravi shouted. "Like you're on a swing! We'll grab you!"

"I can't! I'll fall... and die!" Lewis shouted, his feet dangling less than a metre from the ground.

"No, you won't," Leo said. "The only thing you're going to die of is embarrassment."

Some of the team laughed. Jordan looked like *he* wanted to shove Leo off the platform.

"That's enough, Leo," Mr McKlop said. "I'm warning you-ho-ha-CHOO!"

Back on the trapeze, Lewis's face was turning from white to red with the strain of holding on.

Mr McKlop moved forward to help but down in the bog, Sergeant McCradge held out a hand signalling him to stay put.

From the launching platform, Janek surveyed the scene with his bright blue eyes. He snatched the first trapeze bar from Private Patterson and swung out.

"Hey!" the attendant shouted. "You're supposed to wait until the person has reached the other side!"

Calum and Leo watched Janek hurtle towards Lewis.

"What are you doing, Janek?" Jordan blurted out in a high-pitched squawk.

Lewis tried to look over his shoulder, but it was just as well he couldn't. All he would have seen was the soles of Janek's big feet flying towards him.

Janek lifted his feet to either side of Lewis's hands on the bar and gave the trapeze an almighty shove with the full force of his long legs.

The rest of the team finally understood what he was up to.

"Careful!" Lewis squealed as Jordan and

Ravi grabbed at his waist to pull him onto the landing platform.

Janek swung back to the starting platform, jumped towards it and landed in a crouch.

The whole team let out a cheer. Even Sergeant McCradge looked impressed.

"*That* was the only bit of teamwork I've seen so far," she shouted at the team. "Now, if the rest of you rookies disobey one more order today, I will make you do star jumps until your eighteenth birthdays."

Archers!

"This time!" Lewis offered his encouragement to Jordan.

The rest of the squad watched, bored, as Jordan drew back the sucker-tipped arrow in his bow, breathed out slowly like he was in a movie, and let fly.

The arrow completely missed the big red target, which stood seven metres away. It seemed Jordan was as good at firing arrows as he was at shooting footballs. All the other targets had arrows right in the middle of them – shot by Lewis, Ravi and Ryan.

Ravi sighed.

"Just 'cause you got lucky with your first one!" Jordan shouted at his friend.

"Archers!" Sergeant McCradge shouted. "Remember, this is all about focus. If we don't support each other, we distract each other."

Jordan put another arrow in his bow and fired it, this time without all the showmanship.

It hit the outer ring of the target. Just.

"YES!" Jordan screamed.

As Lewis, Ravi and Ryan all cheered with relief, Fraser barged forward for his turn, hopping up and down with excitement. "I love archery!"

"Calm down, wee man," Private Patterson said. "Wait for the last group to collect their arrows." He snuck a look at his phone before handing Fraser, Calum and Leo their bows.

But Fraser had already grabbed an arrow from the box on the ground. He lined it up in his bow and pulled back the cord.

"Err, Fraser, you'd better wait, dude," Leo said.

Fraser nodded but stayed in position with his arrow drawn back. "I just want to line this up."

Suddenly, a crazy ringtone on Private Patterson's phone shattered the silence of the woods. Everyone jumped, including Fraser – his arrow twanged from his bow and arced in slow motion through the air.

Ravi and Lewis watched in disbelief as it sailed towards Jordan, hitting him right on his bum.

"ARGH!" Jordan dropped to his hands and knees and covered his head in fright. The arrow stuck up from his bottom like a car aerial.

"What're you playing at, wee man?!" Private Patterson hissed at Fraser.

Jordan slowly uncurled himself to see what had happened. When he was confident that no more arrows were flying his way, he stood up.

"I'll pull it off!" Lewis said, running to his friend's aid.

"Leave. It. Lewis." Jordan was snarling. He reached back and yanked the arrow off his bum. It made a loud sucking noise, like a kiss.

Jordan strode towards Fraser, Leo and Calum, the arrow clenched in his hand.

Mr McKlop moved forward but Sergeant McCradge shot out an arm to stop him.

"Sorry, Jordan, sorry!" Fraser was trembling. "It was an accident. Honest!"

"They... made... you... do... it," Jordan said, pointing at Leo and Calum. He was so angry it was hard for him to get each word out.

"No we didn't!" Leo puffed out his chest. "Why don't you guys just run ahead and leave the rest of us to complete the task. Y'know, like you've been doing all day."

"Fraser didn't mean it, Jordan. It was a total accident," Calum offered.

"You're always trying to make fun of me. Make me look stupid!" Jordan was getting upset.

"Calum's right, Jordan – Fraser didn't mean it," Ravi said, appearing at Jordan's side. "Let's go and check out the next obstacle so we can show them how it's done."

Jordan stared at Leo, Fraser and Calum for a couple of seconds longer before throwing the arrow at their feet and storming off.

Goodbye Caleytown F.C., thought Calum as he watched Jordan's crew jog away.

Mudface

Calum flew face-first from the zigzag bar into a grim puddle of cold Scottish mud.

"Eugh!" He spat gritty soil from his mouth and tried to push himself up.

"A-ha ha ha ha ha!" Jordan, Lewis and Ravi were doubled over with laughter at the end of the obstacle. Even Mr McKlop and Leo were trying to suppress grins.

Calum tried to smile and push himself up. The front of his uniform was shiny with wet mud.

He could even feel it seeping into his pants.

"Come on, rookie," Sergeant McCradge shouted without sympathy. "Get back on that bar!"

Calum did. He even made it a few metres along before his soggy trainer went one way and the rest of his body went the other. He fell flat on his back in another puddle of slimy brown mud.

"Up, up, up!" Sergeant McCradge chipped in with her support, signalling to Calum's teammates to join her. They were laughing too hard to help.

"You're totally caked!" Leo pointed out, when Calum finally got to the end of the bar.

"Really? I hadn't noticed," Calum said, mud dripping from his chin.

"Man... you... totally... sucked... at... that!" Jordan managed between belly laughs.
His crew were delighted too.

Calum desperately wanted to pull them all

into the mud. Jordan was right – being made fun of didn't feel good.

A short jog later, the team arrived in front of what looked like a few goal nets stitched together and pinned to the ground.

"What are we meant to do with this?" Jordan asked.

"What do you think, rookie?" Sergeant McCradge said, her rope-like ponytail swinging across her back. "Get down on your belly and crawl under it!"

"But we'll get covered in mud," Jordan protested.

Calum felt the drying mud crack on his cheeks as a smile spread across his face.

"Atten-TION!" Sergeant McCradge shouted, lifting the edge of the net and staring at Jordan until he crouched down on the ground.

"You lot need all the help you can get, so listen up." Sergeant McCradge looked round the reluctant squad. "If you stay close to each other as you crawl under this net, it will stay off the ground and help your fellow soldiers behind you."

Jordan's crew joined him on the ground, ready for the whistle. Calum, Leo and Fraser fell in behind with Janek, Max and Ewan ready to crawl in after them.

PEEEEEEEEEeeeeeEEEEEEP!

Jordan's crew flew under the net like their tails were on fire.

"Come on lads... let's leave these suckers behind," Jordan shouted. They commando-crawled as fast as they could to open up a gap, causing the net to sag in front of Calum and his friends.

"This is… ugh, meant to be a… ugh, team effort," Leo grunted.

The only response he got was a loud fart from Lewis and sniggers from the rest of Jordan's crew.

"Oh, thanks very much…" Leo shouted, wincing at the smell. "We needed that!"

Calum glanced up through the net to see Mr McKlop shaking his head. He looked tired.

"Let's... ugh, at least let Janek, Ewan and Max stay close to us," Fraser piped up.

"Frazzler's right," Calum said, tugging on Leo's trouser leg.

Leo slowed down and they crawled as a team of six to the end of the net, to find that Jordan's crew had already moved on to the next obstacle.

"Great teamwork, Jordan," Leo muttered.

Calum nodded, the stench of mud all around him. It didn't seem like Mr McKlop's plan was going to work.

12

Capture the Flag

In silence, Leo, Calum and Fraser ran all the way to the next obstacle, where Jordan's crew were mucking around in the centre of a clearing.

"What are they up to?" Leo asked.

Jordan, Ryan and Lewis had lifted Ravi into the air.

"Almost, ALMOST!" Ravi flapped at a flag, which was fluttering high above the ground, suspended between two trees.

As Ravi reached up, Lewis lost his balance and the four of them came crashing down to the ground. "Listen up, rugrats!" Sergeant McCradge arrived and planted her feet shoulder-width apart, completely ignoring the four boys sprawled on the ground. "You're on your own with this one.

You'll need to combine all of your tiny brains for this challenge, and your bodies too."

With that, she took Mr McKlop by the elbow and led him to the tree line to watch.

PEEP!

"*On your hands and knees, grab the flag from the pole.*" Fraser read aloud the instructions from the painted sign near the obstacle. "But it's too high to reach if you're on your hands and knees!" he said, his eyes bright and questioning.

"Well, duh, Fraser," Lewis said. "That's what we were trying to do."

"Ease off." Calum stood up for his friend.

"Any bright ideas then, 'star striker'?" Jordan crossed his arms and looked at Calum.

"I dunno, do I?!" Calum hissed.

Jordan took a step forward but was halted by the sound of his watch beeping angrily.

"Well, good luck getting scouted for King's Park Athletic without a team to play for," he said, pointing to his watch. "Our forty-five minutes are up, big head."

Jordan's words ate up the last of Calum's patience. The team had failed in its mission – he could say whatever he wanted now.

"You're the big head, Jordan!" he shouted. "You've always been the big head on this team!"

"Yeah! Plus you and your crew let Battlehill score a goal against us," Leo joined in.

Mr McKlop strode forward from under the trees, but once again Sergeant McCradge shot out an arm to stop him. From over the treetops came the sound of birds flying.

"No, I DIDN'T!" Jordan shot back. "You just think that because you reckon you can do everything better than me!"

"ENOUGH!" An unexpected voice brought the argument to an end.

Wild Geese

One by one, the team turned to see who had shouted.

It was Janek.

He pulled his hat off to reveal bright blond hair and stood, straight as a pine tree, staring at everyone with steady blue eyes.

"Look up there," he said, pointing at the birds honking in the sky.

Everyone raised their eyes to see huge flying Vs of birds passing overhead.

"Before we moved to Scotland, my granddad told me about these birds," Janek said. "They're geese."

Everyone was still in shock that Janek had spoken. He never joined in arguments. Even Mr McKlop looked surprised at the turn of events.

"They fly for thousands of miles every year in that special V formation," he continued.

"So what?" Jordan said, but Janek ignored him.

"My granddad told me that they take turns to fly at the front of the V to break the wind for their friends."

"How does your friend breaking wind in your face for thousands of miles help you?" Jordan asked, smirking at his crew.

For once, they ignored him too.

Janek met Jordan's eyes with a level gaze. "They don't *break wind*, they break *the* wind. Their friends fly in their slipstream."

But Jordan wouldn't give up. "Whatever, Janek. You might not have noticed, but we're footballers, not geese. We can't fly..."

"Shhh... I think I know what Janek's getting at!" Fraser said, his round eyes lighting up.

"Don't shush m—" began Jordan.

"*Shush*!" This time it was Ravi who stopped him. "Let Janek speak."

Jordan was too surprised to answer back.

"We can form a V, just like the geese," Janek said. "That's how we get the flag."

Janek directed three of the biggest players to kneel on their hands and knees in a row on the ground before joining them. Calum tried not to laugh at the bizarre sight of Jordan, Ravi, Max and Janek getting down in the mud under the flag.

Next, Janek told Ryan, Lewis and Calum to climb on top of the bottom four players to form another row of human bricks.

"Wait!" Leo said excitedly. "Are we building a pyramid, Janek?"

"Exactly!" Fraser beamed on Janek's behalf. "*On your hands and knees, grab the flag.* Sergeant

McCradge said it'd take all ten of us to complete the challenge!"

A ripple of anticipation went through the group.

Ewan climbed up to form the third tier of the pyramid, helping Leo up behind him.

"Sorry for not passing to you in the Battlehill game," Leo said as he knelt on top of Lewis's back.

"Likewise, mate," Lewis grunted from under Leo's left knee. Then he turned to glance at Calum next to him. "Sorry for not trying harder when your shot hit the post, Cal."

"No problem, Budgie," Calum said. "Sorry for not squaring it to you in the first place."

"Can we stop giving each other cuddles up there and get on with it?" Jordan grunted from the bottom tier.

Fraser clambered eagerly up the three tiers. He got to the top, knelt on Ewan and Leo's backs and reached for the flag with his right hand. He almost toppled over but just managed to grab it before steadying his momentum.

"YES!"

"Bravo gentlemen, bravo." Mr McKlop came forward to help Fraser down. "Now do you see what you can achieve when you all work together?"

The tiers of players got down before the

boys at the bottom stood up, groaning and trying to brush the mud off their hands and knees. It took Janek a moment to realise that Jordan was holding up a fist for him to bump.

"Well done, captain," Jordan said.

"Right, let's follow Sergeant McCradge back to basecamp," Mr McKlop shouted. "I'm freezing."

The boys fell in behind their coach and he jogged them to the finish line, as a team.

The Field

A few days later, Caleytown were at Fieldling Primary getting changed for their next match. Mr McKlop had stuck the Scotland Stars match report from their Battlehill game on the walls of their changing room.

HOME NEWS LEAGUES PLAYERS CALENDAR

CENTRAL WILDCATS LEAGUE

Caleytown bicker as Battlehill score a barrage of goals

In a deluge of rain, Caleytown's hopes for the Scotland Stars season were almost washed away as they suffered a shock 4–0 defeat. They only had themselves to blame. The home team's constant bickering left Battlehill twins Ric and Nic Catenaccio scratching their heads.

"... was like they *wanted* us to win," Ric said after the

"Come on boys!" Jordan shouted. He was wearing a thermal polo neck and tights under his strip. "Let's not make ourselves look stupid again!"

Calum pinched Leo's arm before he could make a smart comment.

"Ah-ya! What was that for?" Leo yelped.

Janek pulled on the team's brand new captain's armband, grabbed their match ball and led the team out of the changing room. They hadn't really had a captain before, but Janek deserved the honour.

"Man, it's freezing!" Ravi yelped, as they pushed through the fire doors under a sign that said:

WELCOME TO THE FIELD

It was an accurate name for Fieldling Primary's home ground.

"Are we meant to play football on this or plant potatoes in it?" Leo asked, staring at the churned-up grass and rolling fields all around.

At the far end, the pitch sloped up sharply at one corner and the goal posts were rusty. A sheep was munching grass in the box.

"What the...?" Ravi whispered.

"Hey Ravs!" Jordan laughed. "Looks like you'll have a friend to keep you company during the match."

The sheep looked up at Jordan and pooped right in front of the goal.

"Ugh... no way!" Ravi said, instinctively putting his hand up to protect said his quiff.

"Sorry, lads!" said a man in a tracksuit top and old rugby shorts – Fieldling's coach.
He chased the sheep off the playing area.

"Interesting mascot," Mr McKlop said, jogging up behind the squad. He'd shaken off his cold and finally taken the tag off his new tracksuit. "Right, gentlemen, huddle round. Here's the team."

TEAM FORMATION:

Ravi (goal keeper)

Jordan (defence)

Janek (defence, C)

Ryan (right wingback)

Lewis (midfield)

Leo (left wing)

Calum (striker)

SUBS: FRASER, MAX, EWAN

"Before you go out there, I just want to say how proud I—"

Mr McKlop's team talk was interrupted by ten shouting voices. Fieldling came thundering out of their school changing rooms and charged onto the pitch like a herd of cattle. They'd brought a rugby ball with them as well as a football, and kicked both up in the air. The smell of Deep Heat came wafting over on the breeze.

"Listen up, gentlemen," Mr McKlop continued. "This isn't going to be easy, so play for each other, and whatever the result, leave everything you've got out on that pitch. No regrets!"

"NO REGRETS, CALEYTOWN PRIMARY!" Fraser screamed as his team ran on, causing a few of the Fieldling players to stop in their tracks.

The referee called the two nearest players over. Calum ran forward to greet Fieldling's striker.

"Bruce Jacob," the boy said, as he thrust his hand out to Calum. They were the same height, but Bruce's chest, arms and legs were twice the size of Calum's. His forehead hung over his face like a cliff and his nose had a kink in it. "You are?"

"Calum Ferguson." Calum didn't know what else there was to say. He was glad he wouldn't be marking Bruce.

"Aye, well, may the best team win, Calum!"
Bruce Jacob said, and pulled a scrum-cap over
his head, fastening it under his chin.

Who wears a scrum-cap to play football?
Calum thought to himself.

Rough and Tumble

"INTAE HIM!"

One moment, Calum was turning towards the goal with the ball at his feet. The next, he was flying through the air. He landed with a splat and felt cold mud ooze through his strip.

Fieldling had started the match barging, battering and bumping Caleytown about the pitch. But for all that, they were probably the most sporting team Caleytown had ever played.

"You alright... Calum, isn't it?" One of
Fieldling's defenders offered his hand to help
him up.

Calum moved his arms, legs, fingers and toes
to check they were all still working.

"I think so!" he said, taking the boy's hand
and pulling himself to his feet.

Fieldling's keeper gathered up the loose ball and rolled it out to his defence.

"Hit it long!" came the shout from downfield.

Calum looked back down the pitch to see Bruce Jacob thundering through the heavy mud towards Caleytown's goal and waving for the ball.

"My man!" Leo ran towards the defender to put pressure on him.

But in the sludge, Leo couldn't get there quickly enough. The Fieldling player had plenty of time to pick out Bruce Jacob's scrum-capped head.

"MINE!" Jordan shouted, but Bruce got there first and flicked the ball on to his teammate on the wing.

Fieldling's winger ran to where the football had stopped in the mud, and Ravi came rushing out too. It was a 50-50 race.

"Dive on it!" Lewis shouted, from just outside the box.

Ravi started to dive, but, at the last moment, he saw that he was heading for the sheep poo, hair first!

He aborted and clattered into Fieldling's winger.

"Nice tackle!" Calum heard Fieldling's keeper shout from behind him.

The referee was ready to give a penalty but saw Bruce Jacob closing in. "Play on!"

Fieldling's number nine thundered in to smash the ball into the unguarded net.

The Fieldling team surrounded their scorer, shoving him about like they were angry with him.

"Interesting way to celebrate," Leo muttered to Calum, before lifting his boots to pick the mud out from between his studs.

"Let's show them how we celebrate then," Calum said.

Leo smiled. "You're on."

"Good play, Caleytown!" Mr McKlop shouted from the sideline as Lewis found Leo with a great through ball. They were beginning to get the hang of the lumpy, bumpy pitch.

Calum wriggled free from the clutches of his marker and powered towards the front post.

Leo spotted his movement and squared the ball to him.

Calum planted his right foot, kept his eye on the ball, swung his left and...

WHoOSH!

Nothing.

The ball hit a divot of mud and flew up and over his foot. Calum kicked at thin air, spun round and toppled over into the mud once more.

"Why are you Wearing a Scrum-cap Anyway?"

The sheep flopped on its belly to watch Fieldling's winger jog up the slope and stick the ball in a muddy spot for the final corner of the first half.

"Jeez... he's so far uphill his feet are almost in line with my head!" Jordan said to Ravi.

To his left, Bruce Jacob was tightening his scrum-cap.

"Why are you wearing a scrum-cap anyway?" Ryan, Caleytown's right wingback, asked him.

"Never mind that, Ryan! Keep your eyes on your man," Ravi shouted. His quiff shook as he bounced on his toes.

Fieldling's winger ran downhill and smashed the ball as if he was shooting rather than crossing.

Bruce Jacob flung himself head-first at the missile. The ball ricocheted off his cap-protected head and flew through Ravi's quiff on its way into the net.

"That's why!" Bruce shouted at Ryan, as his teammates piled on top of him.

Ravi checked his hair was still there before picking the ball out of the net. Somehow Caleytown found themselves down 2–0.

The ref brought the half to a close and sent Caleytown trudging towards Mr McKlop.

"Great stuff, gentlemen," he said, as he clapped Caleytown off the pitch. With no other spectators there, it was a lonely sound.

"But we're losing 2–0." Lewis said, kicking over a water bottle. "What's so great about that?"

"I've always said that I don't care if we win, lose or draw." Mr McKlop looked at the toppled water bottle until Lewis picked it up. "As long as you're all giving everything you've got for this team – which today, you are."

A light, misty rain had started to fall. A *smirr*, Calum had heard it called. It gave the mud and sheep poo on their strips, legs and faces a whole new stench.

Leo nodded and patted Lewis on the back. "Nice pass back there."

"Yeah, good run, mate," Lewis replied.

Janek and Jordan silently bumped fists to acknowledge each other's handling of Bruce Jacob.

"Now tell me: are you enjoying yourselves?" Mr McKlop stood grinning at them.

The Caleytown players all looked at each other's mud-covered faces.

One by one, bright smiles began to appear.

"I'm having the time of my life, Mr McKlop!" Leo grinned.

"Me too, sir," Ryan said.

"See!" Mr McKlop clapped again. "We're standing about, soaking, on this godforsaken muddy field in the middle of nowhere because we love footba—"

"ONETWOTHREEFOURFIVESIX..." Fieldling's players interrupted Mr McKlop's team talk – again. This time they had formed a big huddle by the side of the pitch and were running on the spot to fire themselves up.

"...SEVENEIGHTNINETEN!"

Finally Fieldling's huddle broke apart and the players started to bump chests and slap each other's shoulders before charging back on to the Field.

"Believe in yourselves, Caleytown!" Mr McKlop cheered as he sent his players to join them.

We're going to need more than belief, thought Calum. Lose this game, and they could kiss the playoffs goodbye.

Just then, a honking noise replaced Fieldling's shouts and grunts. One by one,

Caleytown's players looked up to see where it was coming from.

High above the pitch, huge Vs of geese were flying south across the sky.

Caleytown stood completely still, watching them in silence until...

"COME ON CALEYTOWN PRIMARY!" Janek roared from the bottom of his belly.

Lewis was next, "Come ON lads! Right from the start!"

"Work for each other!" Leo shouted and sprinted on the spot.

"LET'S SHOW THEM HOW GEESE PLAY FOOTBALL!" Fraser screeched.

Calum wanted to roar something too but, like the rest of his team, he was laughing too hard at Fraser's random shout to say anything.

Across the halfway line, Fieldling were staring at them like they were mad.

Best Goal, Ever

Instead of sprinting straight forward from kick-off, Calum chipped a long pass all the way back to Jordan in defence.

Jordan didn't need to control the ball; it simply stopped in the mud for him. He squared it to Janek.

Even on the ploughed-up pitch, classy Janek only needed one touch to control the ball and another one to fire a perfect pass to Ryan on the right.

Long-legged Ryan got the ball under control before tapping it inside to Lewis. With Fieldling players closing him down, Lewis knocked it back to Jordan, who prodded it once more to Janek.

Janek looked up and curled a long pass to Leo's left wing.

Fieldling were chasing after each pass through the swampy mud. Calum could see it was draining their energy.

Leo hit a quick one-two with Lewis to move the attack into Fieldling's half. He looked up and flicked a pass to Calum's feet.

Calum turned with the ball and glanced over to see Lewis' red hair bobbing like a buoy in a sea of mud. He found him with a simple tap.

"Brilliant play, Caleytown! Brilliant!" Mr McKlop shouted from the sideline. But his team wasn't finished yet.

Lewis pushed forward and faked a shot, while Leo ghosted in behind Fieldling's heavy-legged defenders for a cheeky pass.

That's when Calum sniffed his chance. He ran towards the goal then sharply back towards the penalty spot, forming a V in the mud with his tracks, and leaving his tired marker behind.

Leo's cross hit a divot again but Calum was ready for it this time. He jumped horizontally in the air and smashed a volley into the net.

Calum landed in the mud, smiling.

"Let's do that again!" Lewis shouted in Calum's ear as he and Leo pulled him to his feet.

The rest of Calum's teammates came sprinting over to celebrate their best ever team goal, even though they were still 2–1 down.

Over on the sideline, Mr McKlop had muddy patches on the knees of his new tracksuit from sliding along the ground in celebration.

Mud, Guts and Glory

Caleytown had started in yellow and Fieldling in green, but the amount of muck on the pitch meant both teams were wearing all brown as the second half took shape.

"Come on the Geese!" Fraser shouted, as he ran on to replace Ryan. Max came on to replace Jordan too. Their clean strips made them stand out like beacons.

"What's this geese thing?" one of Fieldling's defenders asked Calum. He had mud all over his face.

"It's a long story." Calum shrugged.

Within seconds, Fraser was running at Fieldling's tired defenders with fresh legs. He was so light he didn't seem to leave footprints.

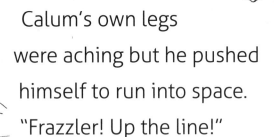

Calum's own legs were aching but he pushed himself to run into space. "Frazzler! Up the line!"

Fraser happily guided the ball along one of the grassier bits of the pitch towards his friend.

Calum controlled the pass near the corner flag.

"That's out!" Fieldling's keeper shouted, but the ref waved play on.

Calum spun and charged at goal.

"On the head!" Leo screamed in the middle.

After days of playing Elevens with Erika, Leo and Sally in the playground, Calum's feet were almost pre-programmed to chip the ball to Leo for a header. He got the ball up and over the goalkeeper, who was rushing straight at him, before...

OOFt!

The keeper plunged his shoulder into Calum's stomach, sending him flying backwards to land flat out on the muddy pitch.

Calum felt like imaginary geese were flying in a circle around his head.

"Sorry, mate, sorry!" the Fieldling keeper apologised. "I forgot which sport I was playing... honest!"

Moments later, Leo appeared above Calum with a muddy ball-shaped imprint on his forehead. "That's three points off the keeper's total."

"Did you score?" Calum attempted to ask, but it came out as, "Di-owa-argh?"

Leo understood though. "Aye, of course!"

Mr McKlop appeared next to Leo. "Are you ok, Mr Ferguson? That was... err, a hefty challenge."

"I think so," Calum said, gasping for breath. Leo, Bruce and the Fieldling keeper peeled him off the mud as if he were a sticker.

"So sorry, mate," the keeper apologised again.

"Aye," Bruce Jacob added, nodding at his teammate, "you know when you've been

tackled by Sunil – that's for sure. I always make sure I'm on his team at rugby."

Calum managed a weak thumbs-up.

"How much time left, sir?" Leo asked the referee.

"About 90 seconds," the ref said.

That brought Calum round like smelling salts. He tried to take a deep breath. It hurt.

"Are you alright to play on?" Mr McKlop asked.

Calum nodded and ran back to his own half to stand next to his teammates. There was no way he was leaving the pitch now.

The Beautiful Game

Despite the hard knock, Calum couldn't remember the last time he had enjoyed a game of football this much.

From the restart, Bruce Jacob whacked the ball all the way back to his defence and ran forward. Leo and Calum galloped through the mud to put pressure on the pass but it was no use. The defender launched the ball like a catapult up to the scrum-capped head of Bruce, who was being marked by Janek.

Bruce slammed into Caleytown's captain, but Janek won the header. Caleytown roared their approval as Max controlled Janek's knockdown and sprayed the ball out to Fraser.

This is it, Calum thought. *This is it!*

The injury Fraser had suffered against Battlehill seemed like a thing of the past as he sped up the pitch. Fieldling's players huffed and puffed after him but it was no use.

"Inside, Frazzler!" Calum croaked as loudly as he could.

Fraser almost lost control of the ball but still found Calum with a pass before getting barged over the sideline.

"Give and go, Cal!" Leo's hand shot into the air.

Calum chipped the ball towards his friend, who controlled the ball on his chest and volleyed it back into Calum's path.

The ball splatted on the penalty spot like an egg hitting the kitchen floor.

Once again, Sunil came charging out of Fieldling's goal to meet Calum. With the memory of their last collision fresh in his ribcage, Calum rushed his shot before leaping out of the keeper's way.

Sunil spread himself,

and...

... *just* blocked the shot with his foot.

The rebound fell to Leo, who hit a first-time curler over Sunil's body.

Calum watched the ball sail goalwards...

CLUNK!

The rebound came back off the bar...

That's it! All this for a draw. Calum couldn't believe it.

Everything went silent.

Calum got back to his feet and desperately made his way to the loose ball, but Bruce Jacob knocked him sideways as he ran past.

What's he doing back here? Calum thought.

That's when he heard someone else arriving on his other side.

squelch,

squelch,

SQUELCH,

SQUELCH!

Calum turned round, half expecting to see the sheep running towards them. Instead he saw Janek's blond hair...

BANG!

Janek smashed the ball at Fieldling's goal.

His shot hit Bruce Jacob square in the stomach.

"YESSSS!" Janek roared as the ball and Fieldling's captain both landed in the goal.

The referee blew his whistle for the end of the game.

PEEP, PEEEEP, PEEEE-EP!

Caleytown had won 3–2!

With some effort, the team toppled Janek to the ground.

Janek shoved them off, his white teeth shining against the brown gloop on his face.

Great goal, Janek!

Where did you appear from?

'Mon the geese!

Calum found himself face-to-face with Jordan, who was as muddy as everyone else.

His thermal tights were ripped at the knee.

"You alright?" Jordan asked.

"Just about. You alright?" Calum asked, pointing to his ripped tights.

"Never better." Jordan smiled.

Both players turned round at a sudden explosion of noise. Fieldling had formed a human tunnel at the side of the pitch and were clapping and shouting.

"It's a guard of honour, gentlemen," Mr McKlop said. "You're supposed to walk through it."

As Fieldling's players slapped him on the back and shouted in his ears, Calum thought to himself, *It doesn't get any better than this.*

"Tough Game, Was It?"

Later that night, Calum was sprawled on his couch next to his mum and Leighton. He could hear his dad muttering and clanking around in the kitchen. The mud from Calum's kit had done something funny to the washing machine.

"You're half asleep, Cal. Good game, was it?" his mum yawned at him.

"The best ever!" Calum yawned back, and meant it – especially after everything the team had been through.

Caleytown were now in with a real chance of qualifying for the Scotland Stars Central Wildcats playoff against their rivals, Muckleton. If they qualified, those two matches would be incredible.

His mum's phone vibrated as a text came through. Seeing it was from Leo, Calum grabbed the phone and read the message. (Calum wasn't allowed his own phone until high school, so Leo had to text his mum. It was really embarrassing.)

"Can I go and read the match report?" Calum asked, pointing at the message.

Round-up on Scotland Stars!!!

"Course you can," his mum said.

Calum struggled to get up from the couch and hobbled over to the computer with Leighton in tow.

He was still sore but he couldn't wait for his next match.

DANNY SCOTT, a die-hard football fan, works for Scottish Book Trust and is the goalie for Scotland Writers F.C.

ALICE A. MORENTORN is a children's book illustrator and a teacher at Emile Cohl School of Arts in Lyon, France.

NATIONAL SOCCER SEVENS TOURNAMENT
CENTRAL WILDCATS LEAGUE

ROUND-UP FROM MATCH DAY FOUR

Caleytown kept their playoff hopes alive with a brave second-half display at the infamous Field, the home of Fieldling Primary. Somehow, 2–0 down at half-time, they dragged themselves to victory with goals from Calum Ferguson, Leo Nkwanu and Janek Powolski.

Over at Muckleton Primary, the league favourites continued to prove everyone right with a dominant display at home to St Catherine's Primary. A first-half hat trick from Kyle Barclay, and two second-half goals from Jack Stark sealed an impressive victory.

It seems at least one playoff contender is confirmed but who will face them? Will it be Battlehill or plucky Caleytown? Caleytown will no doubt be hoping that their local rivals Muckleton can overcome Battlehill in round five: a game that will be broadcast live on our online channel.

MATCH DAY FOUR RESULTS

HOME			AWAY
Fieldling Primary	2	3	Caleytown Primary
Muckleton Primary	5	1	St Catherine's Primary
St Joseph's Primary	4	3	Brawsome Primary
Battlehill Primary	2	0	St Catherine's Primary

LEAGUE TABLE

TEAM	MATCHES WON	MATCHES DRAWN	MATCHES LOST	GOALS SCORED (F)	GOALS AGAINST (A)	POINTS
Muckleton Primary	4	0	0	18	5	12
Battlehill Primary	3	1	0	7	0	10
Caleytown Primary	3	0	1	10	10	9
St Joseph's Primary	2	0	2	13	16	6
Brawsome Primary	1	1	2	12	15	4
Fieldling Primary	0	2	2	8	11	2
Hornbank Primary	0	1	3	5	10	1
St Catherine's Primary	0	1	3	7	13	1

RUMOURS & GOSSIP

⚽ Unconfirmed reports suggest that Caleytown's coach Iain McKlop took his team to Assault Cross to help his players rediscover their team spirit after their ill-tempered collapse against Battlehill Primary. Will it help them hold their nerve if they meet notorious pranksters Muckleton Primary at the next round?

⚽ A shock playoff defeat against Loch Hill Primary sees celebrated team from Castle Rock out of the running for the Edinburgh Knights league. We wonder how Hibs prodigy Brandon Cramond will take the news?

Email: fitba@scotlandstarsfc.co.uk for your thoughts on the action.

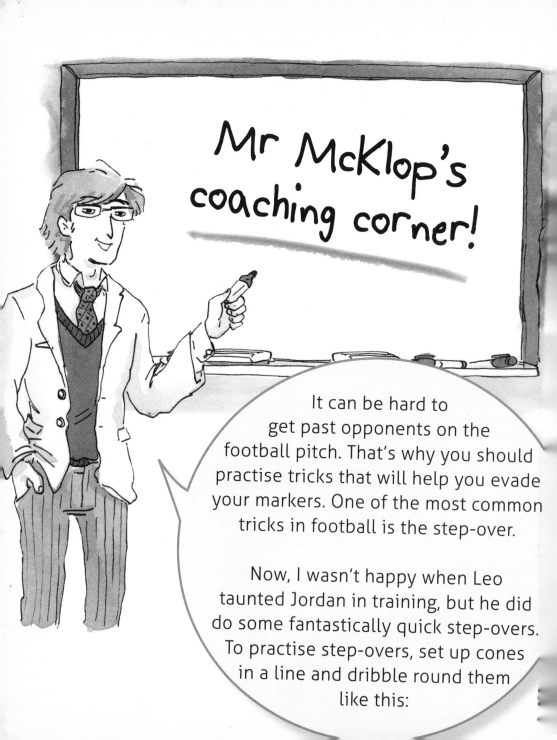

 Step-over

1) Dribble up to each cone and pretend you are going to flick the ball past it with your right or left foot.

2) Instead of flicking the ball, step over the ball with your kicking foot.

3) Push off the foot you stepped over the ball with and flick the ball past the cone with your other boot in the opposite direction.

4) At the next cone, repeat the move the other way around.

5) When you get really good at getting past the cones, try a double step-over! Step-over with one boot, then the other, before flicking the ball past the cone with your first foot.

Step-up your game

To really fool your markers, dip your shoulder on the side you're stepping over with. For example, if you are stepping over with your right, dip your right shoulder.

GRAB THE WHISTLE

1. A shot hits you (the ref!) and goes in. What do you do?
a) Pull your top over your head, run to the corner and celebrate
b) Restart with a dropped ball
c) Award the goal

If you were the referee, would you make the right call?

2. A player's shot hits a beach ball that a fan has thrown onto the pitch. The shot bounces over the keeper and goes in! What must you do?
a) Award two goals if the beach ball goes in too
b) Give a free kick to the goalkeeper
c) Award a goal to the attacking team

3. On a windy day, a goal kick is blown straight back into the goal. What do you do?
a) Award a goal
b) Give a corner
c) Give a round of applause

Answers: 1c, 2c, 3b